NORAH'S ARK

A STORY BY ANN CARTWRIGHT

ILLUSTRATED BY REG CARTWRIGHT

To our parents and to Roy Key

A Red Fox Book

Published by Random House Children's Books
20 Vauxhall Bridge Road, London SW1V 2SA

A division of Random House UK Ltd
London Melbourne Sydney Auckland
Johannesburg and agencies throughout the world

First published by Hutchinson Children's Books 1983
First published in paperback by Puffin 1985

Red Fox edition 1994

Printed in Singapore

RANDOM HOUSE UK Limited Reg. No. 954009

NORAH'S ARK

A STORY BY ANN CARTWRIGHT
ILLUSTRATED BY REG CARTWRIGHT

RED FOX

NORAH lived at Puddle Farm. It was a small farm and Norah and the animals were happy living there except for one thing: the pond was too small. Every morning the animals rushed to the pond and started quarrelling about who was to use it first.

'We want to swim,' said the ducks and geese.

'I need a drink,' grumbled Cow.

'And I want to roll in the mud,' snorted Pig.

'Be quiet all of you,' said Norah. 'You will just have to take it in turns.' But she knew they were right. The pond was too small and there was nothing she could do about it.

ONE night, when the animals had quarrelled even more noisily than usual, Norah thankfully put them to bed in the barn. But as soon as she was gone they tiptoed out to the farmhouse window to watch television.

As they waited for their favourite programme, the weatherman suddenly interrupted with an urgent announcement.

'Here is a flood warning,' he said. 'Tomorrow there will be severe storms and flooding in Puddle Valley.'

'Oh dear!' said Cockerel. 'I do so hate the rain. It makes my feathers soggy.'

'Hooray! Hooray!' shouted Pig. 'Lots of mud for me to roll in.'

As the animals returned to the barn the first small, dark cloud drifted across the sky.

THE next day the sky was full of clouds and the animals were very worried. Crow built a roof over his nest; Goose and Owl flew to the top of the highest trees; and a magpie flew off with Norah's umbrella.

'You won't catch me getting wet,' he cawed.

'Strange how the animals can tell when it's going to rain. You would think they had seen the weather forecast,' thought Norah, as she anxiously paced up and down the farmyard. She had to think of a way to save the animals from the flood. Suddenly, she stopped. 'A boat! That's the answer!' she cried. 'A boat would save us!'

'Come with me,' she called to the animals. 'I need your help. We must turn the old barn over to make a boat!'

She lined them all up and harnessed them with ropes.

'When I say heave, pull as hard as you can. Heave! Heave! Heave!' shouted Norah as she started the tractor's engine.

Pig snorted and Goat groaned. Cow puffed and Henry the dog panted. Even Owl flew down from the trees to help. Suddenly there was a loud crash and the barn rolled over onto its roof.

THAT night, while the animals slept, Norah worked alone in the pouring rain. She nailed planks of wood together for the walls and used the canvas cover from the haystack to make a roof.

Bang! Bang! Bang! Norah's hammer echoed across Puddle Valley far into the night.

It seemed no time at all before Cockerel crowed, 'Time to wake up.' Norah had not even been to bed. Wearily she stopped work and went into the farmhouse.

When the animals saw the boat, Pig and Goat wanted to rush straight on board.

'Just a minute,' barked Henry. 'Stop worrying about yourselves and give Norah three cheers for her hard work.'

Norah was so happy when she heard the cheering that she didn't feel tired any more. She splashed across the water to finish work on the boat.

As she hammered in the last nail, she cried to the watching animals, 'Let's call our boat Norah's Ark.'

And Norah's Ark it was.

THE time had come to go on board. 'Round up all the animals,' Norah told Henry. 'We must make sure no one is left behind.' She sang to herself as they splashed on board:

'The animals went on one by one.
Goat, Pig, Donkey, Owl,
Goose, Duck, Magpie, Fowl.'

When they were all safely on board, Norah relaxed in her comfortable chair and ate some of her favourite tomato sandwiches. She was just falling asleep when she felt the ark begin to move and gently rise. Norah's Ark was afloat.

Cockerel was the first to wake next morning. What he saw made him quite forget to preen his feathers. All around the ark was water. The only land to be seen was the distant hilltops.

PIG'S round body trembled with fear. 'Oh no!' he moaned. 'I'll never see mud again.'

Norah patted his large pink back and whispered to him to be brave or he would frighten the others.

'There's nothing to worry about,' she said to all the animals. 'Let's make this a holiday afloat and when the water goes down we will find our way home.'

'If it's a holiday, I'd like to spend it on grass,' Cow complained.

A few minutes later, the ark reached a hilltop.

'It's your lucky day,' Norah told Cow. 'You can stop here and we'll pick you up later.'

'Wait for me,' Goat squealed. 'I want to come too.'

Norah put down the gangplank and the two animals went ashore.

The ark drifted on between the hilltops and, as they reached each one, Norah let more animals out to graze. When they were all ashore, Norah lay in the sun, while the ducks and geese had swimming races round the ark.

THE ducks won most of the races.

'Race you to Pig's Island,' they shouted to the geese. But as soon as the ducks neared the island they realized something was wrong. Pig was in trouble.

'Help me! Help me! I'm stuck in the mud,' he shouted.

The ducks rushed back to tell Norah the news. She flung up her arms in despair.

'Quick, Henry. You'll have to pull us to Pig's Island.'

'Silly Pig,' Norah said as they struggled to haul him up out of the water. He looked so muddy and funny, that all the animals laughed as Norah washed him clean.

'Let that teach you a lesson,' Norah scolded. 'We nearly lost you. We had better find out how the others are getting on.'

POOR Henry had to drag the ark to each of the hilltops. First they found Sheep, who had eaten so much rich green grass that she couldn't even move. Norah had to carry her on board.

At the next hilltop the strangest sight met their eyes.

Cow was standing in the water and Goat was hanging on to her tail.

'At last you've come,' said Cow. 'Goat is trying to pull my tail off.'

'I'm only holding on so Cow won't be drowned,' Goat protested, as they clambered back on board.

LAST of all they reached Donkey's Island. 'I don't like it here. There's no one to talk to,' he cried.

'Well, you're not alone now,' said Norah, as Donkey carefully picked his way up the gangplank.

All the animals agreed that it was good to be together again.

HOW much longer will the flood last?' asked Cow.

'No one knows,' said Norah, who was secretly worried. To cheer everyone up she suggested a game of 'I Spy'.

'I spy with my little eye something beginning with O,' said Cockerel.

'That's my letter. O is for owl,' Owl said. 'I spy with my large round eye something beginning with W.'

'Water,' all the animals cried at once.

'I spy with my little eye something beginning with TA,' grinned Norah.

'That's not fair,' Pig said with a frown. 'Animals only know words beginning with one letter. I give in.'

'We all give in,' they chorused.

'Television aerial,' said Norah, pointing to the television aerial of Puddle Farm that was sticking out of the water. 'Look, the water must be going down. We'll be home by morning.'

THE next morning, when the animals woke up, the flood had disappeared. It had left behind the biggest pond the animals had ever seen.

'It's like a dream come true,' said Norah, watching all the animals as they happily shared the pond. She blinked her eyes — perhaps it was a dream. But no, there sat Pig at the edge of the pond, covered from head to toe in mud. He looked up at Norah and grinned.

She laughed and the animals joined in until the valley echoed with the sounds of their happiness.